Chester and Bodhi
by Sue Abuelsamid
pictures by Jamie Cosley
color assist Tyler Cosley

Published by Bug Love Books
a division of NyreePress Literary Group
P.O. Box 164882
Fort Worth, TX 76161
www.nyreepress.com
www.buglovebooks.com

ISBN-13 paperback: 978-0-9906662-6-4
ISBN- 13 hardcover: 978-0-9909652-1-3
Juvenile Fiction / General / Animals
A New Home for Bodhi and Chester /Sue Abuelsamid

PRINTED IN THE UNITED STATES OF AMERICA

Bodhi and Chester are golden retrievers who lived in a nice old brown house with a red door, in a small town with their human mom.

There were mountains all around, and trees and flowers and many, many wonderful things to smell, like flowers and raccoons, and apples and plums from trees in the backyard.

Every morning Bodhi and Chester would go for a hike in the mountains where they could roam free and run with all of their other dog buddies.

They would chase deer and even bark at black bears. There were berries to eat. They loved snacking on the red berries they'd find along the trail. On a hot day, Bodhi and Chester would cool off in the streams and lap up fresh water.

And when it rained there were mud puddles to splash and roll in. Bodhi and Chester loved being in the mountains, because they were free to do almost anything they wanted.

At home they had a big yard decorated with a lot of leafy trees and a fence to keep them safe from cars going by.

Bodhi and Chester had so much fun together in their yard. They'd dig holes, chew on sticks, or just dream of rabbits and other adventures. It was the perfect life for a dog.

At night they'd snuggle up near their mom
and rest for another day of exploring.

They loved each other and their mom very much and always looked out for one another.

One day mom began to put things in boxes.
All the funny coloured things in the cupboards
and those that were hanging on the walls started
to disappear.

Though they found that a little weird, mom was still there, and so was the sofa that they love to nap on and all of their toys and their beds, so everything was still okay.

Then something strange happened. One day some men came and took away just about every single item in the house.

That's when Bodhi and Chester grew nervous. Where was everything going? Where was the sofa they love to nap on? And where was the big bed they loved to snuggle in with mom?

All that was left were some blankets on the floor, their two dog beds, and their food and water dishes.

The house even sounded different when Bodhi barked. There was no carpet beneath their feet anymore. But mom was still there so they still figured everything was okay.

The next morning they all got into the car with mom and drove around town, stopping at different houses that they had all been to before. Neither one of them wanted to get out of the car for fear of being left behind. People they knew kept coming out to the car and petting them and looking sad. But they were with mom so everything was okay.

They drove all day long, stopping every so often to stretch their legs and have a drink of water. They didn't recognize anything at the rest stops, but they were with mom, so everything was okay.

Finally, after many hours of driving they arrived to an unfamiliar place with bright lights, lots of traffic and strange sounds. The car stopped in front of a house they had never seen before and they all got out.

Mom said this was their new home, but they didn't understand so when they went inside the empty house they sniffed everything and then settled down in the their beds, snuggling as close to mom as possible.

The next day the same men that had taken all of their things away before began to bring it all back. Familiar smelling boxes arrived, and the sofa where they loved to nap was there, and all of their toys too.

Things were beginning to feel normal again, until they went outside.

Everything outside was new. There were a lot more cars than they had ever seen. There were strange dogs.

There was a big river with water that flowed very fast. There was a very loud and scary machine that raced by and mom called it a "train." They had never seen a train before.

Instead of running free in the mountains, they were both attached to leashes so they couldn't roam very far on their own, or chase anything at all. But mom was there, so everything was okay.

This new place sure was different. There was no shady yard with a fence around it, no play dates with their dog friends.

There were no deer, or bears, either.
But there were sticks to chew on, and
many new things to see. And mom was
there, so everything was okay.

Every day they piled into the car and went for a short drive to a huge park where they could run free, without their new leashes.

There were always other dogs there,
and people with treats in their pockets.

After it would rain, there were
puddles to roll around in.

There were hills to run up and down, grass to eat, many new and delicious smells, rabbits to chase, and other dogs to wrestle with.

It was different, and they missed their old friends, but after some time Bodhi and Chester made new friends and had new adventures. Mom was there, and they were all together, so everything was okay.

$1 from the sale of each book will be donated to Canine Cancer Research or Animal Rescue.

Dedication Page

This book is dedicated to Chip, who helped me realize that life is much better with a dog in the house; to Chester who taught me that the golden years can be incredibly beautiful; and to my little clown Bodhi, for making me laugh every single day.

CPSIA information can be obtained at www.ICGtesting.com
Printed in the USA
LVIW01n0503061114
412207LV00001B/1